Amelia's
CROSS-MY-HEART,
HOPE-TO-DIE

GUIDE

TO THE
REAL, TRUE YOU!

by Marissa Moss
(and all guidance from Amelia)

Simon & Schuster Books for Young Readers

New York   London   Toronto   Sydney

This book is dedicated to Joan Lester —
she doesn't need a guide to know herself!

SIMON & SCHUSTER BOOKS FOR YOUNG READERS
An imprint of Simon & Schuster Children's Publishing Division
1230 Avenue of the Americas, New York, New York, 10020
Copyright © 2010 by Marissa Moss

SIMON & SCHUSTER BOOKS FOR YOUNG READERS
is a trademark of Simon & Schuster, Inc.
Amelia © and the notebook design are
registered trademarks of Marissa Moss.

For information about special discounts for bulk purchases, please contact Simon & Sch
Special Sales at 1-866-506-1949 or business@simonandschuster.com.

The Simon & Schuster Speakers Bureau can bring authors to your live event. For more
information or to book an event, contact the Simon & Schuster Speakers Bureau at
1-866-248-3049 or visit our website at www.simonspeakers.com.

A Paula Wiseman Book
Book design by Amelia
(with help from Tom Daly)

No fonts
or typefaces → The text for this book is hand-lettered.
were harmed   Manufactured in China
in making   1209 SCP
this
book!   2 4 6 8 10 9 7 5 3 1

CIP data for this book is available from
the Library of Congress.

ISBN 978-1-4169-8710-9

first
edition

me?
↓

↑
me?

me?
↙

Some days are like this — I look in the mirror and I don't recognize my own face. I mean, I know it's me, but it's like I'm looking at a stranger, and I'm thinking "That's me? That's really me?" If I had a different face, would I still be the same person? And what do people see when they look at me? What kind of person do they think I am?

And, more important, what kind of person do I think I am? If I had been asked that yesterday, I would have given a whole list - funny, smart, not really cool, but a good artist, fair, basically nice. But something happened today that made me feel not so sure about all that, like maybe I'm not the person I think I am.

It all started when my science teacher, Mr. Engels, asked me to write up my science fair project for the school newspaper.

Okay, it wasn't just _my_ science fair project. I had two partners — Sadie, who turned out to be a nosy jerk who read my PRIVATE, KEEP-OUT notebook, and Felix, who slept through the whole thing. I mean, he _really_ slept, even when the judges came by to check out the science fair exhibits.

Sadie — looks sweet and innocent, but ISN'T! ➔

NOT my idea of real partners at all! ↙ ➔

Felix — looks like an ad for a mattress company ⬅

Mr. Engels said that the school paper wanted a story about our project because it showed how you could end up with results that weren't AT ALL what you predicted — the opposite, I thought, of a successful project, but I guess it makes a funny story.

When he asked me to write the article, I assumed that's what he meant. Me, by myself, with no useless partners to worry about. I admit that when he said "you," he could have meant "you three" or "you plural." But that's the problem with "you" in English. Unless you're from the South and say "y'all," there's no way to tell if "you" means one person or _more_ than one person.

Anyway, I went ahead and wrote a summary, making it as funny as I could so the project wouldn't sound like a total loser (making _me_ sound like a total loser). I didn't bother to talk to Felix or Sadie about it because Felix was good for nothing but snoozing and Sadie was someone I didn't like and didn't trust — not after I caught her snooping in my not-to-be-seen-by-anyone-but-me notebook. After all, the partnership was _over_ and I didn't owe either of them anything.

But the day the paper came out, Sadie came up to me at lunch and exploded.

Hey! We were supposed to write that story together! Mr. Engels said so!

YOU STOLE my project from me like a thief! You're totally unethical, a real, selfish creep, hogging all the credit!

I was stunned. And then I felt horrible. My stomach was all queasy. Because I knew that as ugly as Sadie's words were, they weren't entirely wrong. I had to admit I should have talked to her about the story first. It was rude and definitely not nice to shut her out like that.

But I didn't say any of that to Sadie. I felt like fish, opening my mouth with nothing coming out.

Carly didn't have that problem — she had <u>lots</u> of words.

← she's a great friend to defend me like t

You have a <u>lot</u> of nerve calling Amelia creepy and unethical! You snooped in her notebook! That's about as creepy AND unethical as it gets!

I thought Sadie was going to cry, but she didn't bacl down. "This is between me and Amelia. You can just butt out!" Then she stomped away.

I felt even <u>more</u> horrible. "Carly," I said, "thanks for sticking up for me, but I have to admit Sadie was right in a way."

"She was not! I know you! Maybe you made a mistake — we all do — but you're not an unethical creep!"

I wanted to believe Carly, but I couldn't shake an icky feeling deep down that Sadie had good reasons to be furious with me. Just because she was creepy to me didn't mean I should be creepy to her. Was I trying to get revenge without even knowing it?

That really creeped me out! I needed to know the cross-my-heart, hope-to-die truth about myself. I could only think of one way to discover the real, true me — quizzes! I decided to make a notebook of quizzes that will reveal the nitty-gritty, warts-and-all me. When I'm done taking the tests, I'll really know myself, the deep, mysterious parts along with everything else. I don't mean simple stuff like what's my favorite color or food, either. I mean things like "What's my worst nightmare?" "What kind of friend am I?"

I'll map out my whole brain — from jokes to how brave I am (if I'm brave at all, which I kind of doubt).

I'll see if there are any dark corners of revenge-seeking or nastiness I need to clear out.

Mom says you don't really know a person until you travel with them. Once you get people away from their homes and routines, you see their best and worst qualities. She says she should have known things wouldn't work out with my dad when he wanted to go camping for their honeymoon and she wanted to relax at a fancy beach resort. I know what she means. I could tell Carly would be a great best friend after we went on the science field trip weekend together. We just meshed!

QUIZ #1:
WHAT KIND OF TRAVELER ARE YOU?

If you answered mostly a's:

You're easy-going, open to new experiences, and ready to have fun. You're my kind of traveler! Carly picked all a's just like I knew she would.

If you answered mostly b's:

You'll get frustrated because when you travel you can't control everything. Sometimes you can't control ANYTHING and that would drive you crazy. You're like my sister, Cleo. She expects the red carpet to be rolled out for her every time she steps off a plane.

If you answered mostly c's:

You're a timid traveler and the slightest thing can ruin your day. You expect things to go wrong, but that doesn't make you more prepared, only more anxious. You're like my friend, Leah. She's easy and fun to be with EXCEPT when she travels — then she's awful!

a's idea of luggage- as little as possible. ↙

b's idea of luggage- I can't leave home without my favorite slippers and shampoo. ↓

c's idea of luggage. take ALL you can!

You need to be prepared for ANYTHING!

From that test, I proved I'm a better traveler than I thought, so that's one good thing about me. I can handle long lines, lost luggage, barfing babies, cramped airplane seats, so long as I get to go someplace interesting. I'm actually willing to put up with a lot. So why is it _so_ hard to sit at the same dinner table as Cleo? Why does every little thing about her drive me crazy? Why does Sadie rub me the wrong way when she just _looks_ at me?

Maybe she feels the same way about me and _that's_ why she called me unethical. Not because it's true, but because pet peeves can be small but seem HUGE.

SCALE OF PET PEEVES

Cleo singing-off-key, of course	← So infuriating, you become a raging maniac.
Cleo eating	← You try, try, TRY to remain calm, but you just can't.
Sadie's constant stream of questions	← Hard to ignore, like a dripping faucet.
teachers who give pop quizzes	← Peskily irritating, like a pebble in your shoe.
how the last bit of cereal in the box is always a pile of crumbs	← Mildly annoying like a low buzzing noise in the background or seeing the same commercial ten times in a row.

QUIZ #2:
WHAT DRIVES YOU CRAZY?

Bzzzz z z z z z z z z z z z z z z z z z z z z z

If you answered mostly a's:

It doesn't take much to annoy you. A fly buzzing near, the smell of old, sweaty socks, a loose thread on your shirt and you've had it. Maybe you should start doing yoga so you're less tense.

If you answered mostly b's:

The standard irritating stuff gets to you. Carly is like this. She can stomach a lot, but once she reaches her limit, watch out!

If you answered mostly c's:

You're like me — practically nothing bugs you as much as the obnoxious behavior of someone like Cleo. Really, after being around her, I can put up with almost anything EXCEPT her! I don't know if this makes me more ethical or less creepy, but it does make me more tolerant. I expect Sadie would be an a-type person, the kind who's ready to over-react.

oh, yeah, just try me!

Pick a fight — I'm ready!

When Carly saw me writing in this notebook, making quizzes, she thought I was being silly, that I was taking Sadie way too seriously. She said I didn't need a quiz to tell me who I am — I should already know that. But sometimes it's not so clear to me, especially when something happens that makes me doubt myself.

Hasn't that ever happened to you? Like you think you're being especially generous but everyone else thinks you're stingy, or you go out of your way to do something nice for your mom and she's annoyed instead of grateful, as if your idea of "nice" isn't the same as hers. I think I'm ethical, but Sadie clearly doesn't.

That made Carly think.

Okay, I get what you're saying. But I still think you have to have a strong sense of yourself that doesn't change according to other people's opinions. You have to believe in yourself.

In fact, that should be your next quiz — what are the character traits I have that I think are the most important?

I liked that idea. That's what I want the quizzes to do — help me be clear to myself. So here's the next one:

Please turn page

QUIZ #3:
RATE YOURSELF—WHAT MATTERS MOST TO YOU ABOUT YOU?

ⓐ Doesn't matter at all.	ⓑ Counts some, but not enough to stress about.	ⓒ Really, REALL matters.

① Being smart.

② Being pretty.

③ Being strong.

This isn't a mostly a, b, or c kind of test. It's a quick overview of what you care about most. Maybe it's sports, being organized, and being cool. Maybe it's creativity, being smart, and being strong. Like all the quizzes in this notebook, there are no right or wrong answers. But I realize there are some important questions I didn't include. There's nothing about fairness or honesty or being trustworthy. Does that mean those things don't matter to me and I'm unethical like Sadie said?

No, that's not true. They _do_ matter to me. In fact, they matter so much, I take them for granted. After all, wouldn't EVERYONE say fairness and honesty are good? The question is, when is it okay NOT to be honest? When is lying something I'd do? That's what my next quiz should be about.

← How much do you lie? →

A little?   A lot?   A HUGE amount!

QUIZ #4: THE LYING QUIZ—
BE HONEST ABOUT YOUR LIES!

If you answered mostly a's:
You're a very honest person, maybe even too honest. I'm not an a, so I guess I'm not as ethical as I thought, but I'm not bad, either. I'm human.

If you answered mostly b's:
You're basically honest, but when lying will save you from trouble, you have no problem with it. This is how I answered, so I'm back to where I started — seeing myself as mostly ethical, but not completely. Is this the kind of thing where there can be a gray area? Aren't you either honest or dishonest, good or bad? I guess it's not always so simple.

If you answered mostly c's:
Lying is too easy for you. You lie so much, even you don't know what's really true or not! At least I'm nowhere near this bad.

But I'm still left not sure about myself. I need a better quiz, something that really tests my inner goodness.

Something like how big is your halo?

QUIZ #5:
HOW DO YOU HANDLE CONFUSING ETHICAL SITUATIONS?

If you answered mostly a's:

You're highly moral, with a strong sense of personal responsibility. You're my hero! Actually I answered mostly a's. Okay, I admit there were a bunch of b's too, but no c's, and the majority was still a's. So, ha! I am SO an ethical person, Sadie! This proves it!

If you answered mostly b's:

You have a conscience, but you need to listen to it more. You're on the right track if you want to be.

If you answered mostly c's:

You don't care at all about what's right, just what's good for you. You need to think about other people more — a LOT more.

I showed this quiz to Carly. "See," I said. "Proof positive I'm not a creep like Sadie says."

Carly laughed. "What about the last question? You skewed the ⓐ answer, so you could choose it. That's not exactly fair."

Tell you what — I'll make a test like this and you can answer it. Then it'll be fair.

QUIZ #6: (written by Carly, drawn by Amelia) MORE CONFUSING, ETHICAL SITUATIONS

Carly's right — these are tough questions and sometimes there is no one right answer. That's her point, I guess, that sometimes you have to do your best without knowing for sure what _is_ the best.

Still, I'd say that if you answered mostly a's, you generally feel that if in doubt, tell the authorities. That could be right, but it could also mean being a rat-fink. It all depends...

If you answered mostly b's — and I did — you're not always sure what the right thing to do is. You try to be fair and honest without hurting anyone even though sometimes that's impossible. I don't know if that means I'm good, bad, or confused.

If you answered mostly c's, you have no problem worrying about doing the right thing. You choose whatever serves you best. Sometimes that's a good thing, but only by accident. Still, I have to admire someone who's so decisive. Being a b-type person feels so wishy-washy uncertain.

Carly laughed when I told her that.

I told you it's not so easy to know what's right.

You just have to trust yourself even if you make the wrong choice sometimes.

Those questions were fresh in my head when I saw Sadie at school the next day. She looked as mad at m as ever. I took a deep breath and walked up to her.

Listen, Sadie, I'm really sorry about the newspaper story. You are absolutely right, I should have included you, and I'm asking the paper if they'll print a correction giving you credit for the story.

Apology NOT accepted!

I was shocked again. I thought I was being nice. I w taking the blame, admitting I'd done wrong, and offerin to repair the damage. What more was I supposed to do

Unfortunately, Sadie was ready to tell me EXACTL what to do.

You think you can waltz up to me and make everything okay with one lame, little "I'm sorry"? Well, I don't think so!

You owe me BIG TIME! I put up with you giving me the cold shoulder when I read your stupid noteb and that was an innocent mistake, malicious like you were. Now it's your turn to be punished!

Now I understood! This wasn't about me being ethical or unethical. And it wasn't about me getting revenge. It was about Sadie getting revenge. First she'd wanted to be my friend, then when I got mad at her for snooping, she'd been desperate to get back on my good side. Since that didn't work, she must have seen my mistake as her opportunity and decided to get even. That was a different story! Now I didn't feel guilty at all anymore. Maybe I'd been inconsiderate, but I wasn't vicious, like Sadie said.

It was Sadie who was vicious. ➔

She was frothing at the mouth practically like a rabid dog! ⬅

There was no way to answer her. I just left. When I saw her in science class later, I was careful to not even look at her. She thought I'd given her the cold shoulder before? Now it was going to be the ice blockade!

At lunch I told Carly about Sadie's attack. She wasn't surprised. She said she'd always thought Sadie was ~~weird wierd weird wierd~~ weird.

People who get those quick, intense crushes can just as quickly turn on you and become a nasty enemy. You need to stay as far away from her as possible.

I need a million spelling quizzes to get this word right

Too bad she's in my science class, so I can't stay _that_ far away, but I'll do my best.

"At least I don't have to feel bad about myself anymore," I said. "I know _I_ did the right thing. I apologized. That made it her turn to be gracious and accept it. Instead, she chose to go ballistic!"

Carly nodded. "You don't have to worry about hurting her feelings now. You've done your best."

I thought about that. Had I done my best? Did I have anything to feel guilty about?

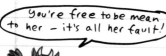

You're free to be mean to her — it's all her fault!

Just because she's nasty doesn't mean you should be

I really tried to be honest with myself. So far, I felt I'd been okay to Sadie. Yeah, I'd made a mistake, but I'd truly, sincerely, honestly apologized. Now what mattered was what I did next. I could be mean back to her, saying she deserved it, or I could listen to the angel in my head.

I didn't want to be a doormat so I wasn't going to be all nicey-nice, but I wouldn't be mean either. I'd trust my instincts, like Carly said. After all, it matters most what _I_ think of myself.

It's funny, when Cleo calls me names, it's easy for me to ignore her.

Don't be a coward, Amelia!

Other people are another story.

Sometimes you're such a creep!

I need to remember to follow my own instincts, to trust how _I_ feel about something. Just because someone says something about you doesn't mean you have to believe it.

So I made a quickie quiz about whether following your gut is a good or bad idea. Before I take Carly's advice and trust my instincts, I want to know I'm usually right!

If you picked mostly a's:
You need to rely on something other than your gut feelings. Or you need to develop some strong instincts. Right now your choices are based on chance more than anything else. Maybe try a Magic 8-Ball.

If you answered mostly b's:
Your instincts are pretty good — you can depend on them most of the time.

If you answered mostly c's:
Your instincts are right on target and keep you from getting into too much trouble. Congratulations!

I'm more of a "b" than a "c," but that's good enough that I can trust myself. I think since I apologized to Sadie, I don't owe her anything else. She may think I still have some making up to do, but that's _her_ opinion. I don't have to agree with it.

Sadie should rely on the → Magic 8-Ball.

NOT AS I SEE IT.

← Then she'd understand I'm not a creep.

I showed Carly my new quiz. It shows I know what she means — I need to trust my own sense of things

"It's good," Carly said. "But knowing yourself, trusting yourself, is way more important than any test can measure." Then she told me something she'd never said to anyone before.

You have to promise you won't repeat this because it really embarrasses me even though it's totally stupid and not even true.

Of course, I promised. I'm good at keeping secrets.

This happened in 5th grade, before we were friends. Some girl passed me a note in class. It was the first time anyone had done that, and I felt really cool and proud unfolding it in my lap to read.

But when I read it, it was a mean, terrible note. So mean, I almost cried. Part of what made it nasty was that it came out of nowhere for no reason. I barely knew the girl who gave it to me. Why would she hate me that much?

"What did the note say?" I couldn't imagine the awful insult that could hurt Carly enough to make her want to cry. She's such a strong person, I didn't think ANY note could do that.

Carly lowered her eyes as if even the memory of the note might bring tears. "It said I was a lying you-know-what and that I stuffed my bra to get boys to like me." Now Carly looked at me, her eyes flashing anger. "What really hurt was that I didn't even wear a bra then. I was totally flat. And I didn't care about boys. It was ALL a lie, a vicious lie meant to really hurt me."

I put my arm around her. "Plus it was stupid."

"The point is, it DID hurt me, even though it was dumb nonsense. That's what I'm getting at here. Sometimes people say things to be mean, to have power over you. You can't let them."

I was furious at the girl for being so nasty.

But I was even more angry at _me_, for letting myself be hurt by it even for a minute.

Carly sighed. "I should have been stronger then. I'm not saying it doesn't matter what people say about you. I'm saying you have to think about whether _that_ person's opinion matters. Sadie's doesn't, just like the girl who passed me the note."

I remembered my own experience with nasty notes — the ones Maxine slipped into my locker last year.

They made me feel I bad about myself even though I knew they were meant to be poisonous, and I shouldn't pay attention to them.

So the question is, how do you know when to trust a person or not, whether they're a friend or an enemy? Sometimes it's really not clear. You think a kid has your best interests at heart and then suddenly you realize, wait a minute, I'm being set up!

I never liked Sadie, but I thought she liked me, that she wanted to be my friend. And friends aren't mean to you. I need to be able to tell when a friend is really a friend.

QUIZ #8:

OW CAN YOU TELL A FRIEND FROM AN ENEMY?

If you answered a's and b's:

You know a good friend when you see one and you know how to be a good friend yourself.

If you answered ANY c's:

Watch out! That's not a friend — that's an enemy disguised as a friend. They're not as rare as you might think and they're way worse than straight-out enemies because they PRETEND to be your friend. That's what makes them dangerous. You know not to trust an enemy, but a fake friend, that's different. You can easily make the mistake of trusting them. DON'T!

That's what Sadie was — a fake friend. Now that I've figured that out, she doesn't bother me at all.

Today in science, I even forgot to avoid her when we took turns with the micro-scope.

Turn the knob to focus.

I know

I was just being helpful.

She seemed surprised I said anyth[ing] to her.

I guess I'm feeling more confident about trusting myself. And Carly's story about the nasty note really struck me. I mean, she's a strong, smart person, but a lying, mean note got to her. So, of course, Sadie's yelling at me would be upsetting. Because that stupid rhyme we learned in kindergarten is SO not true — Sticks and stones may break my bones, but names can REALLY hurt me!

Or they used to. I'm getting stronger, like Carly. I know it all depends on who's doing the name-calling. Sadie saying I'm a creep — that I can shake off and ignore. Now if Carly said that, it would be something else. I'd have to believe it!

That's what my last quiz should be about, figuring out whose opinions really matter, who you should listen to.

I already know answer #1: ME! What I think about myself really matters! →

Still, I also know I make mistakes some times. Like at first I didn't like my dad, but then I got to know him better. But that was about him — not me.

Or maybe the final quiz should show what I know about myself, a guide to the real, true me. I think I'll just trust my instincts and see what kind of quiz comes out.

QUIZ #9:
WHAT DESCRIBES YOU BEST?

There are no right answers, just a sense of who you are, what makes you happy, sad, or scared. What makes me happy is that I don't have to worry about Sadie anymore. The last few days she hasn't even glared at me. I guess she got tired of being so angry (it's exhausting, I know!).

I did my part – I got the student newspaper to print a correction so Sadie and Felix got credit for the story about our project.

Not that Felix noticed – he slept through it, like he sleeps through everything.

zzzzzz

But at least I knew I'd done the right thing – and Sadie knew.

I thought I was done with quizzes, but after school yesterday, Carly suggested I make one last test so I'd have a nice, even ten of them.

How about a quiz on quizzes? A test on tests?

"Huh?" I asked. "I don't get what you mean."

"Well," said Carly, "you've done practically everything else, but you haven't asked how people handle tests themselves. And that's such a BIG part of school now, all those stupid, standardized tests."

She had a point, but my quizzes aren't those kind of quizzes, not the fill-in-the-bubble-with-a-number-two-pencil kind of test. Besides, those tests are the OPPOSITE of fun. I want mine to be fun!

I'm good at school tests, but I don't like them. →

Especrally the "apple is to tree like cereal is to toilet" kind of questions - I HATE those!

"C'mon! If anyone can make a test about tests fun, it'll be you," Carly said.

Of course, after that I had to try. So here's my last, last quiz. It's not about the real, true you, but the test-taking you.

QUIZ #10:

THE TESTS TEST OR QUIZ ON QUIZZES

If you answered mostly a's:

You take tests seriously and try hard to do well on them, sometimes too hard. Relax and have a little fun! Make your own tests and give them to your friends. You'll see how it feels to be on the other end of a quiz.

If you answered mostly b's:

You're careful and calm when it comes to tests, but you can still be thrown by little things like a pencil that snaps or someone chewing gum nearby. You need to have more fun! Try making your own tests for your family and see who scores the best. Remember, you get to do the grading.

If you answered mostly c's:

You have problems taking tests seriously. Yes, you have more fun than most people, but I wonder about your grades. Maybe you need to take some tests, like the ones person "a" and person "b" are going to make. And next time, try!

I forgot to include the question, what do you absolutely have to have with you when you take a test? ⓐ your rabbit's foot

ⓑ your lucky pencil   ⓒ a BIG eraser

Now I'm all quizzed out, at least for a while. I know how I travel, handle sticky, ethical situations, lie or don't lie. I know what drives me crazy and what matters most to me about myself. I even know how I handle quizzes - both making and taking them.

The next time someone says something about me that doesn't feel right, I'll trust myself.

I may not have x-ray vision, but I don't need it to see myself clearly.

And no one else has as good a view of me as me.

Today in French, Carly slipped me a note. I unfolded it in my lap so I could read it without the teacher seeing. It said:

You passed the test!

I smiled at her, but I'm not sure what test she means. One of the quizzes I made here? Dealing with Sadie? Learning to trust myself?

It wasn't until after school that I had the chance to ask her. "What kind of test did you mean?"

Carly grinned. "I meant all of them, really. You figured out how to use tests to learn something — not to check what you already knew. I think that's pretty cool. I mean, all our lives we take these different tests to prove to people how much we know about math or history or spelling, that kind of stuff. We take tests to rate ourselves and how well our schools are teaching us."

"But I think those tests are a big waste of time," Carly went on. "Every minute spent taking one is a minute spent NOT learning. Except with YOUR tests. I discovered something about myself every time I took one — and they were fun!"

It's funny you say that because you're the one who helped me see myself more clearly — more than any quiz.

That's what friends are for!

She was right! You need your friends to understand you. If they don't, how can they be real, true friends?

I guess I owed Sadie — a non-friend — some thanks for starting everything. Or not. I should give myself some credit for turning her sour lemons into lemonade. She can have credit for the science fair project but that's all.

That shows how I know myself now. But there someone else I know almost as well, someone w deserves credit for these quizzes, this noteboo and lots more.

I hugged Carly.

Thanks, but what did I do?

You stood by me. You got me when I couldn't see myself.

You even figured out my quizzes before I did

And most of all, she helped me be MORE myself. I don't need a quiz to tell me that makes an A++++ friend. Those are the friends who see you for who you really are, and when you're around them, you're at your best. They help make you more of whoever you're meant to be — and those are rare friends!

Carly's like that for me. I trust my gut on that one